PERFORMANCE CRITERIA

CYBORG DESIRES

REAGAN HAWK
MANDY M. ROTH

RAVEN HAPPY HOUR LLC

Performance Criteria (Cyborg Desires)
by

Mandy M. Roth writing as Reagan Hawk

Performance Criteria (Cyborg Desires) © Copyright 2016,
Reagan Hawk
First Electronic Printing 2006
Second Electronic Printing March 2016, Raven Happy
Hour LLC
ALL RIGHTS RESERVED.

All books are copyrighted to the author and may not be resold or given away without written permission from the author, Mandy M. Roth.

This novel is a work of fiction and intended for mature audiences only. Any and all characters, names, events, places and incidents are used under the umbrella of fiction and are of the author's imagination and should not be confused with fact. Any resemblance to persons, living or dead, or events or places or locales is merely coincidence.

Published by Raven Happy Hour LLC
Oxford, MS USA
Raven Happy Hour LLC and all affiliate sites and projects are © Copyrighted 2004-2016

Mandy M. Roth, Online
Mandy loves hearing from readers and can be found interacting on social media.
(copy & paste links into your browser window)

Website: http://www.MandyRoth.com

Blog: http://www.MandyRoth.com/blog

Facebook:
http://www.facebook.com/AuthorMandyRoth

Twitter: @MandyMRoth

Book Release Newsletter:
mandyroth.com/newsletter.htm
(Newsletters: I do not share emails and only send newsletters when there is a new release/contest/or sales)

PROLOGUE

Planet Athena in the Epimetheus Quadrant of the A-QET73 System...

BRAD PRIED the bay doors open, his heart feeling as if it were lodged in his throat as thoughts of something happening to Aeron troubled him. He should have never agreed to leave her side. The idea of the higher-ups sending pact members to opposite corners of the galaxy to avoid capture by the Vanos hadn't sat well with him but he'd listened, to a point, respecting the others' wishes. Instead of completely leaving the planet, Brad declined a promotion and stayed on as a captain to assure he would be in the vicinity of Aeron's lab.

It wasn't until he intercepted a transmission leaking Aeron's whereabouts that Brad knew he should have trusted his gut and never left her side. He'd wanted to take her with him and confess all he felt about her. Only one thing had prevented him from doing just that—Conell, her on-again, off-again boyfriend.

None of it mattered now. Aeron's safety was his only concern.

"Aeron," he called, rushing down the corridor towards her lab. The sound of his voice echoed off the walls and was the only response he received. Adrenaline coursed through his veins as he continued full force into Aeron's lab.

"Aeron!"

A quick look around the area showed no sign of her. Brad grabbed the end of a work station and fought for breath. "Aeron, honey!"

"Ouch. Brad, is that you?" Her soft voice never sounded so sweet. She peeked up from behind a tall table, rubbing her head gingerly. "What are you doing here? I thought we agreed to—"

He was on her in an instant, dragging her petite frame against his body and holding her close. She smelled of mint, and Brad knew

Aeron had been playing with her hydroponics garden again.

"Brad?"

"You're safe? Not hurt? Unharmed? All right?" He visually scanned her, searching for any indication she was injured but finding none.

A tiny laugh came from her and tugged at his heartstrings. "I'm fine, but aren't you Captain Redundant. Could you think of any more ways to ask if I'm okay? Want to tell me why you're here?" She pressed her cheek to his chest and he felt the tension in her ebb away. "Not that I'm complaining or anything."

"I need to get you somewhere safe, Aeron," he said, not wanting to let go. Holding her felt right. "*They* know where you are."

She tensed. "How?"

He'd wondered the same thing when he'd intercepted the transmission leaking her location. Brad would have assumed a pact member turned on Aeron if he didn't already know better. Each member was loyal to the cause—protecting humans from an all-out Vanos invasion. Aeron had also been one of the few pact members who remained on the planet Athena. She'd been adamant about not leaving her work behind and Brad had been equally as stern on her going. In the end, Conell stepped in and sided with Aeron, trumping Brad's decision. "I don't know, honey."

Aeron leaned back and lifted her sandy-blonde brows to form a question on her face. "Brad, you're acting strange. You just called me honey."

"Is Conell here?" He didn't have time to worry about slips of the tongue. He needed to get her somewhere safe.

She shook her head. "No. He left, like almost everyone else did."

Anger coursed through Brad's body. As much as he hated knowing Conell held Aeron's heart, he hated the knowledge the man had left her alone more. The pact agreement didn't mean a thing. Not when it came to Aeron's safety. Brad would move the heavens to assure she was safe. "Come on, we need to get you back to your father's ship. Is it still docked in the south bay? The damn techs didn't move it, did they? I know it was on their list."

"Yes, but it's not been serviced in the last six months." She closed her eyes and drew in a deep breath. "I couldn't do it, Brad. Not after they killed him. Being around the ship reminded me of my father too much. It's not ready to fly. Not yet." Aeron's bottom lip trembled as fear crept into her voice. "Brad?"

"Shhh, it's fine, Aeron. Every time you and the others got going on a new theory, I got the hell out of here and hung out on your father's ship. I've kept up on it. In fact, I think it's one of the best vessels out there." Unable to stand the sight of her frightened, Brad leaned his head down and pressed his lips to hers. He waited, stuck in the moment, sure she'd push him away. She didn't. Instead, Aeron parted her lips for him, allowing Brad to ease his tongue in. The kiss was intoxicating, stealing Brad's ability to do anything other than lose himself in the taste of her sweet lips.

The second Aeron went to her tiptoes and slid her hands into the back of his hair, Brad pulled her towards the ground, too many years wanting but never having built up for him to stop. It felt so good to finally have her with him. He wouldn't think about tomorrow, about how she'd no doubt push him away. No. He'd concentrate on the here and now.

Something whizzed past his head and his

military training kicked in. Brad shielded her body with his as shots from a Vanos weapon flew by. He knew the ammunition they packed was often filled with a substance that ate human flesh. Having Vanos blood in him would retard the destruction if he was hit, up to a point. If Aeron was hit, she wouldn't heal.

A beaker exploded, raining glass down on them. Brad kept Aeron tucked safely beneath him. When he realized she hadn't made a sound, his worst fear hit him head on.

She's dead.

"Aeron?" He leaned back enough to look down at her. Her blue eyes were wide as she clung to him.

She peeked out. "Are they gone?"

"No," he said, relief breaking in his voice. "Are you hurt?"

Shaking her head, she whimpered before grabbing his neck and coming away with blood. "You're bleeding!"

"Just a scratch, baby." He planted a chaste kiss on her forehead and then rolled off her. "Stay put."

"Brad." She grabbed his hand. "They'll kill you."

He drew his sidearm and winked. "Not if I kill them first. Promise you'll stay here."

She nodded and he took one last chance to stare at her. Telling her how he really felt for her was on the tip of his tongue but he held back. He'd get her to safety and then tell her once they were airborne. Brad tugged his hand free of Aeron's and forced a smile to his face. "We'll get through this, Aeron."

AERON WATCHED in horror as Brad bolted upright and began firing off shots. The enemy returned fire, a volley of bullets, breaking glass so that fumes from now-destroyed lab experiments filled the room. Each time something popped, Aeron yelped. She rolled to her side and onto broken glass. It bit at her exposed skin but she ignored the pain, too worried about Brad's welfare to mind.

She peeked around the side of the table and came face-to-face with a dead Vanos. Shocked, she lurched back, raking her legs through more broken glass. A portable microbiology system crashed to the floor next to her, sparks popping out of the back of it, and a piece of its glass front flew wide and lodged into her upper leg. The cut, while superficial, resulted in a large quantity of blood. She pulled the shard free of her leg, careful to avoid cutting herself further.

Brad seized hold of her arm and yanked her to her feet. Aeron knew better than to question his judgment when it came to matters such as these. Brad was a soldier and a damn fine one at that. If he wanted to move, she'd follow blindly.

She touched her swollen lips with her free hand, still in awe he'd kissed her. For years she'd wanted him. When it finally happened, their kiss had been explosive.

He led her towards the double bay doors and stalled, just a second, as he raked his gaze over her. "Aeron, you're bleeding."

"It's just a—"

Something loud sounded and she watched in what felt like slow motion as Brad's body lifted off the ground. He fired his weapon towards the doors a nanosecond before he released his hold on it and continued his descent.

It took Aeron's brain a moment to catch up with what she saw—Brad, lying on his back. Torn flesh, deep-bleeding wounds, covered his once unmarred body. The only part still recognizable was his face. Bile rose and she steeled her nerves as she glanced towards the door and spotted a dead Vanos there.

"B-Brad?" She reached out tentatively, already knowing the worst had come true. "No!"

Instinct kicked in and Aeron shut off her emotions, focusing on Brad instead. She launched into the steps necessary to save him, if it were possible, all the while blocking out the sounds of station police heading her way. Help was coming, but for Brad, help was already too late. As his blood coated her hands, she knew she would do everything in her power to make this right.

Bending down, Aeron pressed her lips to his cheek and released a secret she'd held dear. "I love you."

Brad's hand jerked and Aeron dismissed it as nerves, but silently prayed the action meant some part of him could still hear her.

ONE

Orbiting Planet Perseus in the Prometheus Quadrant of the A-QPT45 System…

DR. AERON BRAXTON fastened the cranium chassis closed and pulled the tawny flap of skin that had been grown in fibrin gel down over it. She ran her fingers through the chin-length, silky black hair. By all outward appearances, the area looked like the back of a humanoid's neck. Inside, it was a labor of love, consisting of electronics and organic materials, thus creating a perfect blend—the perfect droid. A little too perfect.

She closed her eyes, needing a moment to

push thoughts better left buried in the past back down. She'd done it again—worked herself to the brink of exhaustion, leaving her vulnerable to memories of loved ones lost.

He's not really here. It just looks like him.

Aeron ran her hands over the back of her creation's neck. It was so smooth, so perfect, that she could feel no difference between it and any other humanoid. No one would be able to detect the difference either, as was the plan. It had been her obsession to produce a race of androids that could pass as humanoids, use them to infiltrate enemy headquarters and to eliminate all threats to human life. Many scientists had tried, but all had failed—at least until now. She'd been given little choice in the matter. Aeron refused to let a good man die in vain—especially the man she loved.

As hard as she tried to suppress thoughts of it all, Aeron couldn't help but look at her labor of love and reflect on the day her world crumbled around her. Years ago, she and a small group of others like her formed a pact, promising one another they would do everything within their power to restore order to the galaxy. Over the years, many of the original group had fallen at the hands of the enemy. The rest were forced to separate, knowing if they remained as a unit they would draw unwanted attention. They had been her everything after her father's death. When her friends were stripped away from her, Aeron felt naked, vulnerable, and had wanted to give up all hope. One man broke their agreement, coming to her anyway, needing to know she was safe. It had cost him his life and she would forever bear the guilt.

It's not really him anymore. He's just a droid now.

She stroked the droid's cheek, keeping her eyes closed. Most of the time, she could separate the droid from the man. On days such as this, the lines blurred, leaving her mourning the loss of the man she'd fallen in love with.

They stole him from me and now they'll pay.

It was high time someone held the Vanos accountable and tipped the scales back in the humanoids' favor. The Vanusimos, or Vanos for short, had steadily taken over the majority of the galaxies on the outer quadrants and were quickly becoming a threat to Star Union territories. The Vanos were humanoid-like. In fact, they looked a great deal like the humans who had descended from Earth, except for their massive size. She had yet to meet one who wasn't pushing seven feet tall. Even the females of the species were tall. Well over six feet, females in general seemed to be rare among the Vanos. This scarcity was one of the reasons humanoid females were kept far from the males, if possible. The Vanos had been known to pillage star ports, destroying any who stood in their path and leaving their mark on the next generation.

Vanos were simply more advanced versions of humans. They possessed greater speed, agility and strength, and healed up to five times faster than a normal human. Combine their size with their additional abilities, and humans couldn't compete. She'd paid dearly for the Vanos DNA she'd blended in with other humanoid varieties while creating her version of her perfect android. He would need to pass as both Vanos and human, something urban legend claimed to be possible. From centuries of pillaging, there were a number of Vanos halfbreeds who tended to avoid drawing attention to the fact they shared direct links with the Vanos.

The Vanos' numbers were great and their

hold on shipping ports unparalleled. Many referred to them as the space mafia. The leader of the Vanos had actually been nicknamed "Don Vanos" over the years. Since their lifespan was longer than the average human, no one was sure how old Don Vanos was. All they were sure of was that he had to be stopped, and a secret society of human rebels vowed to be the ones to do it since the Star Union had yet to acknowledge the Vanos as a viable threat to them. The Star Union was notorious for endless mounds of red tape, so none were shocked they hadn't acted against the Vanos yet. The Vanos hadn't been foolish enough to attack within Star Union Territory, knowing an attack would be taken as an act of war and dealt with promptly.

Aeron was a card-carrying member of the human rebellion and yearned for the day when humans living in the outer quadrants would no longer be under the thumb of the Vanos. Already the rebellion's numbers had tripled. No longer were they just a group of fighters willing to take up arms. Now they also consisted of doctors, scientists and engineers—as well as others—all helping for the greater good. They were nearing a point they could approach Star

Union with enough evidence to hopefully gain their backing, which would help tremendously. The heads of the Star Union had to see the severity of the situation to believe it. Since they would never be caught dead in the outer quadrants, proving there was a significant problem was easier said than done.

Being independently wealthy, Aeron didn't need funding for her research, meaning she didn't have to tell anyone about her project. No one knew about the droid, at least not yet. If he worked, she'd take him before the Rebel Council and the Star Union, should they come on board, to offer his services in helping free the humans on the outer edges from the reign of the Vanos. She'd also have to deal with the backlash that would no doubt come from his appearance.

Walking around to the front of *her* droid, Aeron drew in a sharp breath when she saw the finished product. He was a beautiful specimen of a man, perfect in every way—tall, dark-haired and handsome as hell. Just as the man he was modeled after had been.

Unable to help herself, Aeron let her gaze slide down him, skimming over his lower extremities. Oh, he certainly was perfection at its finest. Too bad he'd have little interest in sex. Even knowing that previous attempts at endowing androids with a sexual drive or the need to procreate had failed, Aeron had still labored over hers, modifying the equipment necessary to partake in sexual acts. It just didn't seem right to create a man, only to rob him of what made him male.

When he was still human, he'd been virile, and Aeron refused to rob him of that because of injury. She'd even gone so far as to add an unbelievable amount of sensors throughout his body that could be turned on and off at will. That way, in the event of torture or injury, the droid could simply shut off any feelings of pain.

The Vanos had set up medical stations at each shipping port on the outer quadrants and were known to yank unsuspecting travelers aside to screen them. Their intent was to weed out android assassins. Having no penis would have been a major tip off he wasn't human any longer. The materials she'd used on her creation all mimicked those used in repairing damaged humanoid bodies. It wasn't unusual for someone to have over seventy percent of their body reworked. With population controls in effect and life expectancies almost double what they had been a hundred years ago, humans and other humanoids were the healthiest they'd ever been—at least those who could afford the treatments were. Many of the posts on the outer quadrant lacked adequate resources for the replacements. Once the Vanos were no longer a threat, she and the other rebels planned to put an end to terror, hunger and sickness, giving the less fortunate a shot at living long, healthy lives.

Glancing down at the object in question, Aeron licked her lips at the sight of his ruddy cock. Even flaccid, it was huge—just the way she liked them. Well, the way she used to like them. Her work had kept her too busy to date, meaning she hadn't known the company of a man in years. Masturbation had been her only outlet. The urge to touch him, run her fingers over his shaft and feel it in her hands was all-consuming. Holding back had become a full-time job.

"Mmm, I should have never left you so tempting. I want to lick you and then climb on top of you." She ran her hand over his dormant shaft. He even felt real—silky, thick and long.

"Just a few more days, Brad, then we'll take

you out and give you a test." She caressed his chiseled chest and grinned. He'd more than exceeded her hopes and dreams for him, and he'd yet to be activated. "Boy, would I ever like to take you for a test drive. Too bad you're an assassin and not a lover."

Aeron had decided to keep the name "Brad" for the droid, as the man he was modeled after had been named. Well, Bradshaw Fairbanks, III, but he only answered to Brad.

So shall my droid.

Turning, she pulled her shirt over her head and worked her pants off. It was already the wee hours of the morning and she'd once again lost herself in her work. She had agreed to meet with a friend from the original pact in the morning and would only get a few hours sleep as it was. Excited didn't even begin to cover how she felt about the arrival of one of the old gang. If she managed to get any sleep, it would be a miracle.

Something flickered out of the corner of her eye and she glanced at Brad, sure he'd moved. A nervous laugh escaped her. "Brad, I think my mind's playing tricks on me. That or I'm so horny my brain wants to give me hope you're more than just the ultimate killing machine." She smiled. "The real Brad would have laughed me out of the room if he knew about you."

Her mood soured quickly as she remembered all the tubes and machines needed to keep a supposed brain-dead soldier alive. She'd sat by his side, refusing to believe he was gone but knowing he'd never be the same. He'd had his own room, complete with all the equipment necessary to sustain him. Seeing a once strong, proud man lying motionless in a bed, day in and day out, tore at her gut. She'd talked to him as if he could hear her and kept him abreast on all the latest happenings, all the while hoping he'd magically awaken. It never happened. The decision to shut Brad's life support off hadn't been her own. Distant relatives petitioned for his life-support system to be shut off—citing his benefits as the reason why.

They were money-hungry bastards who wanted his inheritance and military pay outs. Since they couldn't collect benefits while he was alive, they eventually saw to it the courts were involved in the matter. In the end they won the battle, but she won the war.

Aeron saw to it that Brad's body was left

untouched, praying the slight period of death—one hour—wouldn't make what she had planned to do impossible. As she glanced from her bed to the droid, she knew she'd made the right decision. Even if he were only a certain percent of the man she'd fallen for all those years ago, he still meant the world to her. A piece of him lived on, even if it could never understand or know the truth.

Thoughts of droid Brad being in the field, under fire, filled Aeron's head. No part of her wanted to see the warrior before her harmed, even though it was part of the deal. Brad had ended up brain dead because of the Vanos. Losing the second version of him wouldn't be easy.

Black hair and chocolate brown eyes made the already alluring droid before her downright irresistible. In addition to being sexy and modeled after the man she'd once been close to confessing she was in love with, Brad was also the only person, for lack of a better term, she confided in anymore. It wasn't as if he actually talked back. At least not yet, but he was still someone she confided in. Talking out loud had become a rather bad habit she'd developed over the course of creating Brad.

"You know," she said as she stared at him. "I wasn't always quite as pathetic as I am now. I used to have a life. A good one. Before the Vanos killed my father and my best friend." She took a deep breath, needing to focus on anything other than the topic at hand. "I'm excited about seeing Conell. It's been a long time. Of course, he can't see you. Not yet, anyway. He wouldn't understand."

For a split second Aeron thought Brad blinked. That was foolish so she dismissed it with a wave of her hand. "Brad, I'm on the verge of losing my mind. I need human contact. I can't wait to see Conell in the morning, but I'm a little concerned about my willpower or lack thereof. It was hard enough to resist the temptation of Conell when we attended the University together." She waggled her brows. "I think we both know I buckled under the pressure. I can only imagine how hard it will be to keep my hands to myself now that I haven't had sex in years."

Aeron continued on, talking to Brad as if he could really hear her. "There was a point in my life that I thought I'd be Mrs. Conell Ballou. I'm still not entirely sure what went wrong in our relationship, or even if what we had qualified as one, but I do know that a piece of my heart stayed with him."

She stepped closer to Brad and went to her tiptoes. She was tall for a human female, but nowhere near Brad's height. Force of habit dictated she kiss his cheek lightly and give him a hug. As she wrapped her arms around his body, she fought back tears. "Swear to me you'll be careful. Promise me that you won't go off half-cocked and get yourself killed. I won't know if I programmed you correctly until you're in the field and then it could be too late. I know I can't keep you…that your natural instincts will demand you do your duty and bring down the enemy, but I don't want to let you go."

She sighed, still clinging to him. "As sad as this sounds, you're my everything, Brad. I think Conell and the others will grow to like you too. Not as much as I do, of course, but they'll know how important you are to us all. I'm sure of it."

TWO

Brad waited until he was sure Aeron was asleep before moving. The beautiful blonde woman had been the last thing he remembered seeing after the blast from the Vanos weapon took out his chest, and the first thing he ever registered when she began the process of rebuilding him. He'd longed to tell her how much she'd meant to him. It had been one of his primary reasons for disobeying their sworn pact and coming for her the minute he learned they'd discovered her location. Brad held no regrets. Her life had been worth his.

He'd first met Aeron when they were in their last year of private intermediate schooling. They'd hit it off almost instantly, even though he thought for sure he'd loathe her when he spotted the bookworm, should-have-been cheerleader, sitting in the atrium, studying.

He and his friends had stolen someone's lunch chip and were playing keep-away with it, tossing it just out of the guy's reach when Aeron had looked up, saw what they were doing and charged him. Never had Brad expected the tiny slip of a girl to speak to him, let alone come at him. Sure, he'd hoped. A guy would have to be blind to miss the fact Aeron was gorgeous. She'd not only charged him, but she'd hit him with her reading tablet, cracking it over his head, leaving him love struck.

She also made him apologize to the guy he'd spent the greater part of his life teasing—Conell Ballou. From that moment on, Brad found every excuse he could to be near her. He stopped slacking in his classes and signed up for courses that would keep him near Aeron. It was for the best. He ended up following her to the University to study science. He was recruited straight from there into the military and served the Star Union proudly, always turning down promotions that would leave him having to go far from Aeron.

Right before his accident, Brad declined yet

another promotion, opting instead to remain nothing more than a captain of an outer quadrant base because Aeron had set up a small research lab there with Conell and others like them. He'd of course lied to her, making her believe he'd left the planet. She'd found out what Brad had truly done after his accident. She couldn't be upset with him. Not with the price he paid to keep her safe. He was dedicated. All the pact members were. They were determined to stop the conditions the Vanos were forcing the humans on the outskirts to live in. For a while, they were successful. Once their names were leaked to the Vanos, it became too dangerous for them to remain together. The pact had given each of them walking orders, assuring them a safe haven while Brad remained behind with Aeron. The two had grown close. For some reason, Aeron had always been convinced Brad saw her only as a friend. It wasn't true. He'd loved her from the moment she cracked him over the head with her tablet.

He'd also been an idiot from that day forth, always holding back the truth, always playing the role of best friend instead of lover. When he'd learned the Vanos had found her, he wasted no time getting to her. The moment he'd burst into her research facility, he'd found her on her knees, potting plants necessary for their healing qualities. His entrance had startled her. Not nearly as much as when he kissed her, seconds before the Vanos burst through, opening fire on them. It was actually humane compared to some of the ways the Vanos were known to take lives. Brad had felt pain, but only for a moment. The second he heard Aeron's horrified screams, saw her frantic eyes and sensed her touch, he knew then that she cared. When she pressed her lips to his cheek and whispered "I love you", he made a silent vow to come back to her, in some form or other, right before the darkness fully consumed him.

The darkness had clung to him for what felt like forever, only being broken during the times he heard Aeron's voice, felt her touch. When she'd rebuilt his damaged body and brought him back in a form she often referred to as a droid, the darkness had been chased away. Only to be replaced by the face of the woman he loved.

If anything, Brad loved her more now than he had. Not that he even believed that to be possible. There was something about the way her blue eyes sparkled when she smiled, or how candidly she spoke when she assumed he could not hear, that had made things deep within his body tighten.

Dr. Aeron Braxton had done her job, all right. She'd created the perfect droid, more perfect than even she imagined. Brad had been only days into his rebirth when his neural senses kicked on automatically, tapping directly into his memories. From that moment, he'd watched the entire procedure—how she'd painstakingly labored over every tiny detail of rebuilding him to the way he'd been prior to the attack. Her dedication and determination made the transition into what he was slowly becoming easier.

He'd always been reluctant to admit there was Vanos blood in his family line. It was distant but there. Aeron discovered all about it after the attack. From the endless hours she spent talking softly to him, as if she somehow knew he was still able to hear, he learned that the doctors had wanted to wipe their hands of him the moment they found traces of Vanos DNA. Aeron refused to let them. She even found a way to take him with her.

Gods, I love this woman.

His chest tightened at the thought of holding Aeron the way he'd always dreamed of. Getting to know everything about her over the last few years left his already intense feelings for her bordering on uncontrollable. Her tiny quirks even made him clench his fists after she walked away, fighting the urge to take her then and there. Whenever Aeron was deep in thought, her tongue skated over her bottom lip. Brad longed to run his thumb over the very track her tongue took before claiming her mouth with his own.

The cock which she had repaired in accordance with her deepest fantasy sprang to life—surprisingly enough, her fantasy was exactly what he'd already been packing prior to the attack.

She's always wanted me too.

The thought warmed him.

Aeron continued to torture him, night after night, by undressing in front of him before crawling into the shower or bed. Some nights, she'd lie in bed, put her hand between her legs and work her clit until she kicked and cried out. He'd wanted to go to her, slide his body over hers and sink into her silken depths. He wanted to be the one bringing her pleasure. That was easier said than done.

Each night was harder and harder. The endless waiting, the yearning, the need to bury himself within her and make her his own, but he hadn't been able to. No, Brad needed to work on himself while she slept each night. He'd tweaked her already remarkable settings and enhanced himself far beyond what she'd hoped for, thankful he'd followed her into the area of science all those years ago.

His enhancements were almost complete. He had one small thing to do and then he would claim Aeron as his lifemate—his wife.

Brad walked over to the information download unit and aligned his wireless sensors with it by spreading his hand wide. He mentally commanded the computer to begin the process of downloading any remaining data on human mating rituals by pushing the signal into the unit's central processing unit. He had all the points the good doctor wanted covered, like weapons, hand-to-hand combat, the most effective ways to kill another, basic humanoid interactions, military operations and so on, but she hadn't thought to give him any other information in regards to sex and love. Brad had been a skilled lover of women prior to the accident, but his memories were a bit hazy at times. Only the ones of Aeron were strong. He was confident, but only to a point. The idea of trying to seduce Aeron, only to find himself nervous or a born-again virgin, did not appeal to him.

Brad had stumbled upon the information by accident and had soaked up every morsel of it that he could. It was during the downloading periods he'd learned what a family meant to Aeron and how much he wanted to give her one. She didn't seem to believe he could be both a solider for the cause and a companion, but Brad knew better. He knew without a doubt he could be both a warrior and a lover to her. It was now a matter of proving his case. But first, he needed to insure he could give her everything he could have when he was a human male.

Stepping into the examination chamber, Brad waited for the door to slide shut before doing his final test. He took a petri dish and held it in one hand. Accessing his stored erotic images of Aeron pleasuring herself, Brad took hold of his cock and began working it. Slowly, he slid his hand over the long shaft while visions of Aeron moving her fingers in and out of her sweet core flashed before him. Seeing her finger-fuck herself was too much. He stroked himself harder, faster, until his balls tightened and his body jerked. He set the tip of his dick against the dish and ejaculated over it. Granted, it wasn't the ideal testing situation, but it would do all the same and it felt good to find release, even though he wanted it to be within Aeron.

Gripping the dish carefully, he took a deep breath before he slid it into the chamber. "*Ahh*, computer, initiate a spectral analysis on semen…now."

The examination chamber beeped twice before ejecting the dish. Brad glanced at the monitor and waited with bated breath. A smile crept over his face and he had to fight to keep from shouting out with joy. It had worked. His final test was not only complete, but a success. After months of tweaking, his semen once again carried live sperm. He could make love to Aeron and hopefully create a family with her.

THREE

Aeron sat up and rubbed her eyes. Two hours of sleep wasn't enough. If she wasn't so excited to meet with Conell, she'd have just slept in. The thrill of seeing Conell again after all these years was too tempting to resist. He'd been handsome in school, though a bit on the skinny side. That, along with his tendency to be just as big of a bookworm as her, had a way of leaving him a target for bullies. He was the reason she'd met Brad. Conell was also one of the smartest men she'd ever met. They'd bonded first as friends and then as something more than friends.

Even if her pending visitor wasn't Conell, Aeron would have still been excited. She had to admit that she missed interacting with other humanoids. So far, she'd only had the company of a droid who was non-responsive. Sure, Brad was great to look at, but he wasn't much of a conversationalist. Talking to thin air, while therapeutic, wasn't as rewarding as interacting with another human. Besides, Brad was a killing machine, nothing more. It wasn't as if he'd ever want to sit down and have a heart-to-heart with her like the real Brad used to. No. He was created to be a heartless assassin. Not a best friend.

Stop viewing him as your best friend then, Aeron. He's not that man anymore.

Mentally scolding herself did little to shake the feeling that Brad was the closest person in the universe to her. Rolling out of bed, she stretched her arms above her head and smiled at Brad, who remained silent, as he always did, in the corner of her lab. Why she slept there every night instead of in her actual bedroom was beyond her. At first, it seemed to make more sense. She worked until the wee hours of the morning on him, and putting a bed nearby was logical. After a while, she found she couldn't sleep unless Brad was near her. His presence made her feel safe and less alone in the vast space around her.

"I'm going to miss you when you go, big guy," she said, scratching her breast as she yawned. "The rebellion has such a need for you that I'll never get time to see you. Not that you'll notice or care, but it would be nice if you could stop by and visit me sometime. Hey, if you work out, I could maybe make you a brother or, umm, a female like you."

Aeron nearly choked on her words. The very idea of making a woman for Brad, even though he would lack sexual desires, sickened her. In some weird, twisted way Brad was hers and hers alone. Sharing him wasn't an option.

The computer chimed, indicating someone was attempting to dock on her ship. She glanced at the wall-time unit and cursed. "He's early!"

Naked and barely awake, Aeron ran and grabbed her dirty clothes off the floor. A pair of tan pants and a pink shirt wasn't exactly what she wanted to greet Conell in but they would have to do. The clothing replicator would take at least five minutes, and running up to her bedroom would take longer. Leaving Conell's ship sitting out in space, waiting for her to answer, wasn't an option. The man was a legend in the field of science and wasn't to be kept waiting. Not only that, but she missed him too much to wait another second.

"Brad, this is it. Conell's here." She smoothed her shirt down and raked her gaze over Brad. "It's moments like this I realize how much I need some girlfriends. I almost asked you if I looked all right."

She snickered. "I really need to get laid."

Crossing her fingers, Aeron winked. "Maybe, if I'm lucky, that will happen today. Who knows, Conell might still be single and I'm guessing he's only gotten better with age."

She froze as what sounded like a growl came from Brad's direction. Dismissing the noise, tiredness winning out over better sense, Aeron searched the lab for her boots, but came up empty. Going barefoot was less than professional, but in her defense, he was early. It also didn't hurt that she and Conell had once seen more than the other's bare feet.

She activated the hidden door to her lab and headed out into the control room. "Computer, identify vessel requesting permission to dock."

"It is a personal transport vessel, registered

to a Dr. Conell Ballou."

"Permission granted."

Aeron entered the receiving room and waited for the dock bay doors to open. When they did, she couldn't believe her eyes. Conell, her lab partner, friend and lover from ten years ago, had grown into a striking man. His sandy blond hair flopped down over wire glasses and the faintest hint of a beard appeared on his face. He'd bulked up a good deal since she had last seen him and it did wonders for his physique. He'd been handsome back then. Now he was simply gorgeous.

His gaze met hers and his green eyes widened. "Aeron? Is that really you? You haven't changed one bit in ten years."

"Yeah…umm…hi, I mean, welcome," she stammered, slightly embarrassed. The need to run and hug him was great. She held back.

Conell smiled and took his jacket off. He glanced around her receiving room and nodded towards the direction of her massive white sofa. Designed in a circular shape to fit the living space's dimension, it was said to seat over twenty, but since she'd never actually had twenty guests aboard her vessel, she wasn't sure.

"Nice."

"Thanks," she said, blushing slightly, although she wasn't sure why. "So, tell me, Conell, what in the universe made you look me up after all these years."

He took a step towards her wet bar. "May I?"

"Help yourself, just please don't make any Cosmic Magic Punch or I'll be sick on the spot." She laughed, remembering how sick she'd been after a night of partying. She and Conell had decided to celebrate the fact they'd passed finals. It sounded good at the time. The three days they spent recovering from their alcohol-induced stupor weren't so great.

Conell wrinkled his nose and chuckled. "Ugh, I'm going to pass on the Cosmic Magic Punch too. How about an Orbit Blitz?"

Aeron's breath caught as Conell's green gaze locked on her. The last time she'd had an Orbit Blitz she woke to find herself naked and wrapped around Conell's long body. It had been what finally broke the barrier between them, causing them to cross the line between friends and something more.

Aeron swallowed hard, thinking back to the

nights they'd spent together. "Umm, no. I'll pass but thank you."

Pass? I want sex. No. I need sex. Why the hell am I passing?

She wiped her palm on her thigh and did her best to calm the rush of heat that went to her face as Conell winked.

"It's been too long, Aeron. I miss talking with you. Hell, I miss you period. I hate having to keep my distance."

"I miss you too, Conell." She took a seat and tore her gaze from him momentarily, needing to force herself to breathe. "What brings you way out here? Last I heard you were living it up at the University of Falcierone. I can't imagine ever wanting to leave the place, let alone travel to the outer quadrants. You're free to do as you please with the protection of the Star Union at your back."

Conell shifted awkwardly as he tapped the wet bar controls. "Orbit Blitz please." He glanced at Aeron and there was no mistaking the look of longing on his handsome face. "What will you have?"

"Nothing."

He seemed to pull into himself, avoiding her

gaze. "Aeron, trust me, honey, you're going to want a drink," he said evenly.

"Conell, what's going on? You're acting strange and that's not like you. At least not like the 'you' I remember."

He stiffened and her insides cramped.

She shook her head and sighed. "Don't tell me we did something wild back then and ended up signing a marriage contract. That or you're really a woman."

Conell choked on his drink as he took his first sip. "A woman? No."

Aeron grabbed the edge of the portable table next to her. "We're not married, right?"

Tipping his head, he peered out from emerald green eyes as a sly smile spread over his face. "You look as though that would be a bad thing. Would it? Would entering into a marriage with me be so horrible?"

"That's not what I meant and you know it. Now, what's going on?"

He slammed the remainder of his drink before covering the distance between them. It was difficult to do anything other than visually trace the contours of his body, but Aeron managed to force her gaze to Conell's face.

She'd gone too long without the touch of a man but remembered his well. He had a gentle touch, one of a scientist, but she'd always sensed more to him. Conell wasn't one to take to violence, yet there were times when Aeron had caught glimpses of extreme anger in his eyes, like he was fighting it with all his might.

Conell had never been a ladies man while in university. In fact, he'd been ostracized by many of the other students after rumors of his parentage began to circulate. His six-feet, eight-inch frame had opened the door to vicious rumors about Conell having Vanos blood in him. His brother was rumored to be a bit shorter than Conell but faster and stronger than others at the Star Union Academy. Being part Vanos was a stigma no one wanted attached to their names, least of all a future scientist.

Staring at him, Aeron couldn't help but notice how much Conell had filled his tall body out. She'd accelerated the growth of Brad's organic body parts before halting it so that he'd no longer age at a rate faster than a Vanos. Brad's body and mind were that of a mixed-Vanos male in his early thirties—as the real Brad would have been had he survived. Vanos males tended to hit sexual puberty in their late teens but their bodies took longer to adapt to their size. Often males of the race did not "grow" into their bodies until they were in their mid-to-late twenties.

Questioning Conell as to whether or not he truly possessed DNA from the Vanos wasn't an option. He'd hated each and every time it was called into question.

Conell made himself another drink and looked over at her. "How secure is your ship?"

"How secure? What do you mean?"

Conell glanced around nervously before moving to sit down on the sofa. "Can I speak freely here?"

"Of course."

"Good," he said before taking a sip of his drink. "Aeron, I don't know how to tell you this so I'm just going to say it. The Vanos have put a bounty on the head of any scientist they feel may be a threat to them."

Aeron gulped. *Any scientist?* Although her project was a secret, she was well-known in the field of genetic research. She took great pains to keep her location a secret from them but it was never a guarantee. "Let me guess, I'm on the list."

"Yeah, we both are, along with many of our colleagues. Basically the members of the original pact have now become public enemy number one in their opinion." Conell took another sip of his drink and Aeron suddenly felt the urge for one as well. She resisted. "A friend of mine is on the inside and he smuggled a chip out with all the scientists' names on it. I sent a copy to my brother in the Star Union and then contacted you."

Aeron was quiet for a second, taking time to soak in the severity of Conell's words. Much to her surprise, she didn't panic. In fact, an eerie sense of peace settled over her as she cast him a reassuring look. "You put yourself at great risk coming here and not just fleeing. Why?"

Conell sighed. "I gave in and left you before when it all went down. I heard what happened, how Fairbanks made it back in time to save you but lost his life in the process."

Aeron closed her eyes a moment, fighting the memories wanting to come.

Conell made a low, pained noise. "I hated that it wasn't me there with you, Aeron. I hated hearing how horrible the attack on you both was. I refuse to stay away now. I didn't know it was going down last time or I'd have come." He snorted. "Hell, I'd have never left but you pushed so hard, telling me our relationship had run its course. Then Fairbanks told me that you never really loved me."

She gasped. "Brad said that?"

"I'm sorry I went, Aeron. I can't change history but I can hopefully fix the future. When I saw your name on the Vanos' hit-list, I couldn't bear the idea of something happening to you. I couldn't take a chance that inter-vessel communications are being monitored by the Vanos so I had to come to you. You were always a good friend to me and I thought this might pay that back."

Aeron rolled her eyes and decided on getting that drink after all. "I didn't become friends or your girlfriend to get something out of you, Conell. I did it because you're a nice guy, and at the time, we worked well together—as friends and lovers. You don't owe me anything."

"Aeron, the entire scientific community knows that you're a loner who rarely, if ever, leaves her grand, battle-sized ship, and if we know, then so do the Vanos."

"We appreciate your concern, Ballou, but Aeron's not alone," a male voice said from behind her. "It's good to see you. It's been too long."

Aeron's eyes widened as she turned slowly to see who spoke. Her jaw dropped when she found Brad there, dressed in a pair of black military-style pants and a tight black T-shirt. It molded to his massive chest and matched his chin-length hair.

Brad's chocolate gaze met hers and she didn't move, couldn't move. How could this be? She hadn't activated him yet. And what in star's name prompted him to say what he did to Conell?

Conell's gaze narrowed a second before he stood and took a step back. "Fairbanks? How? I heard you were…"

"I'm not," Brad said, his voice even.

Aeron blinked, thinking it all a hallucination. When she opened her eyes to see Brad and Conell before her, the reality of it all sunk in. The shock, hurt and bewilderment on Conell's face was too much for her to bear. The need to clear up the misunderstanding was great. Aeron shook her head. "No, Conell. Brad's not—"

Brad set his sights on Conell, looking anything but pleased. "Not dead. We thought it best to let the rumor stand to keep the Vanos looking in the other direction. We both knew they wanted me out of the way and had come at her to draw me out. We also knew they'd never let us live in peace if we dared to leak the truth of my existence." His hot gaze landed on her. "I wouldn't leave her then, and I sure the hell won't leave her now that she's my wife."

Aeron stumbled and knocked a glass off the wet bar. *Wife?* What the hell had prompted Brad to say that? Better yet, how in star's name was he mobile?

She stared at him, hoping the answers to her questions would magically develop. They didn't. As she opened her mouth to protest, Brad shot her a hard look. The blood in her veins ran cold and a shiver moved over her.

He was made to be a killing machine, Aeron. Don't push him. He's not the man you knew. He'll kill Conell and you.

Swallowing hard, Aeron tried and failed to steady her nerves. There was no logical explanation for why Brad was up and about. She'd not activated him and he surely couldn't activate himself. Right?

The tension in the room grew to enormous proportions. The urge to grab Conell's hand and run was great. Having programmed Brad, Aeron knew better than to try to escape. He was faster than she could ever hope to be and he wouldn't take kindly to her attempt at fleeing.

"Aeron, are you well?" Conell asked, making a move to come to her.

It was on the tip of her tongue to scream at him to run, but she held back, fearing for his safety. "I-I'm fine. Just shocked to see Brad up and about so soon."

"Is he *still* a late sleeper?" There was a definite note in Conell's voice indicating he suspected something was off, but he didn't verbalize it.

"Something like that," Brad said, his gaze hard and his body tense.

In truth, as frightening as it was to see Brad up and about on his own, he was captivating. Aeron's traitorous body agreed with her mind as her nipples hardened to pebble-like points and her inner thighs tightened. His voice was as deep as she remembered it being and his overall presence as commanding. She'd always known he was a warrior, but Aeron couldn't have predicted what seeing Brad back in action would do to her. She knew she should be terrified, and in truth, part of her was, but the scientist and woman within her shared a simpatico moment—he was a fascinating specimen. Almost as captivating as the real Brad.

"Aeron." Conell's voice was like a bucket of ice-cold water, snapping her out of her stupor and bringing her back to reality.

"Yes?"

"*Yes?* I've been asking you again about your ship's defensive system, but I don't think you've heard a word I've said."

Defensive system? She hadn't heard him utter another word about the ship and its defenses.

Brad crossed his muscular arms over his chest, puffing it out in a display of alpha maleness. "*Our* ship's defensive system is that of Star Union's finest war crafts. I've seen to it myself."

"We have a defense system?" Aeron asked, unable to mask her surprise. Last she knew she had shields to protect from meteorite showers and small blasts, but nothing that could withstand a full-fledged Vanos attack.

Brad's dark gaze landed on her and her pulse sped. "Of course, honey, don't you remember all the time I spent in the command room, under the control panel?"

No.

"Um, right. I think I blocked it to keep you from suffering my wrath. You know how much I hate it when one of your projects takes up all your time."

A slow, sexy smile slid over Brad's handsome face. "Depending on the punishment you had in mind, I might be willing to risk it."

He's flirting with me. And he's good at it. Almost as good as the real one had been.

Heat rushed to her face and she knew she was blushing. Aeron swiped her hand over her forehead, positive she was sweating. Much to her surprise, she wasn't. Still, the entire receiving room seemed to have jumped in temperature.

"I think congratulations are in order," Conell said. "I had no idea the two of you were married, Aeron. In fact, no one I talked to even knew you were seriously dating someone. You two did an amazing job of keeping Brad's existence a secret. Your last name's the same as it was, so I'm sure you can see how I'd miss something as important as—"

"We've been together for years, Conell," Brad said snidely. "Just because we never set our relationship out for the universe to see, doesn't take away from it. In my opinion," he licked his lower lip as he stared at her, "it's only served to intensify our bond. Wouldn't you agree, Aeron?"

She nodded, unable to offer anything more substantial.

Brad smiled. "And as far as her last name not changing, I'm shocked you'd even question that, Conell. Many races of humanoids don't bother with the changing of surnames. In some, the male takes the female's last name as a show of respect to her father should he have no sons of his own, as was the case with Aeron and myself. Since Aeron's father passed away having only had one child, we thought it was a nice way to pay tribute to him—having her use Braxton in public and Braxton-Fairbanks between the two of us. Not only that, but this assures our children carry the Braxton name as well."

Children?

Aeron gulped.

This isn't happening.

Conell drew in a deep breath, fisting his glass as if it were taking everything in him not to smash it against the wall. "You're pregnant?"

She couldn't form an answer to save her life. It was all too much.

Brad didn't seem the least bit bothered. He let out a manly chuckle. "No. Not yet. We've only just decided to start trying."

We did? Funny, I was still debating on when to plug you in.

She watched as Brad closed the distance between them. Her body went rigid as he wrapped his arms around her and pulled her to him. He caressed the small of her back. The action was so human and so reassuring, that for a moment, Aeron forgot who and what Brad now was. She laid the palm of her hand against his chest and relaxed. His touch was oddly comforting, as the real Brad's had been. Shock raced through her as he kissed the top of her head lightly while giving two quick tugs to the back of her hair.

Brad used to do that to me.

"You should have woken me the moment Conell arrived, honey. I've wanted to see him again for years. We talk so much about the old gang, always wondering about their welfare, that I welcome the opportunity to see them again." It was impossible to miss the jealous tone of Brad's voice and the possessive manner with which he held her.

The idea of Brad harming Conell sickened her. It was one thing for the creation to attack the creator, but to turn on her friends was another matter.

Creation?

The word no longer seemed to describe Brad.

She shook her head and touched her temple. "Conell, could you excuse us? I need to lie down. I fear I'm fighting a rather nasty Tochitirion flu bug. We stopped there for refueling a few days back and I think it caught up with me."

His green gaze swept over her, and for a moment, Aeron thought for sure Conell knew something was amiss. She watched with bated breath, fearful he'd do something rash. When he headed towards her, Aeron yelped. Brad caressed the back of her arm, all the while his body tense.

Stepping out of Brad's embrace, Aeron wedged herself between the tall men, silently praying it wouldn't come down to a fight. Brad could and no doubt would snap Conell's neck with little to no effort. She glanced at Brad and pleaded with her eyes for him to spare Conell. His face betrayed nothing.

Conell wrapped his arms around her and hugged her tight. "Take care of yourself, little Aeron. The Vanos have this area of the galaxy mapped out. My brother gave me a set of coordinates in Star Union-friendly territory. I'll upload them to your ship once I return to mine. And I mean it, congratulations on finding out Fairbanks was Mr. Right."

More like Mr. Deadly.

She shook her head and held him tight. "No, stay here…my father had this starship built to house hundreds of scientists and their families. Stay, and we'll head to your coordinates together."

Stay? I've lost my mind. Brad will rip Conell's head off his shoulders.

Conell glanced nervously over at Brad. "I

don't think that would be wise. I get the sense your *husband* wants your undivided attention."

Brad cleared his throat. "Of course I do, but my *wife* clearly wishes for you to be safe and she's right. This ship will hold many."

Relief washed through Aeron when she realized Brad wasn't going to harm Conell after all. Unable to hide her joy, she covered her mouth with her hand and nodded, tears welling in her eyes. "Thank you."

Brad winked, catching her off-guard.

Conell touched her cheek lightly. "Tell you what. I need to warn three more people I know on the list. After I do that, I'll rendezvous with the two of you at the preset coordinates. Maybe, we can get the old team together and put this ship to good use." He backed away and offered a rather forced smile to Brad. She'd seen Conell use the same smile on those he despised during their days at the University. Hell, he'd even cast it in Brad's direction a time or two back then as well.

She held her breath until he'd exited the ship, only to realize she was alone with a droid she obviously knew nothing about.

FOUR

Brad waited until Conell was gone to look at Aeron. She just stared at him with wide eyes. It was cute and a bit unnerving. He thought she would have been happier to see him up and moving around with his memories and emotions intact. He would have waited and let her think that she'd activated him, but his super-human hearing had allowed him to pick up on their conversation. He would not let harm come to Aeron, nor would he allow her to fall into the arms or bed of an ex-lover. She was his and his alone.

"Aeron, are you well?"

"I'm...*uhhh*...Brad?"

A Cheshire cat smile slid over his face as he

took another step towards her. "Yes. Are you upset?"

She shook her head slightly and backed away from him. His sensors detected her blood pressure had elevated and her breathing was shallow. Fear. She was afraid of him.

"Aeron I..." He took another step and she backed away again. "I would never harm you."

"*Pfffttt*," she huffed. "You were designed to kill, Brad. No offense, but the fact you overrode my command codes and are even standing here talking to me is enough to make me a bit uneasy around you. Knowing you could get across the room before I could blink and snap my neck with one hand doesn't really help matters any either."

He had to prove to her he wasn't just an assassin. He was a man. The man she'd confessed to loving all those years ago. "You're welcome to restrain me." Unable to help himself, he smiled. "From the tutorials I downloaded, being tied up looked very appealing. I have to admit to having no real experience there on my own, so I'm open."

Her blue eyes grew wide. "You *are* flirting with me!"

"Of course."

Aeron tossed her hands in the air. "'*Of course*,' he says, as if it's everyday this kind of *dei'geri* happens."

It was rare to hear Aeron curse, but entirely too cute to comment on, so Brad simply allowed her to continue with her mini-rant. The pink shirt she wore hugged her curves as she flailed her arms about, all the while making him painfully hard.

"It's not normal for a droid to turn himself on, Brad. It's not normal for one designed for military use to flirt. And it sure in the hell is *not* normal for one to claim to be my husband."

He nodded. "Yeah, I gathered as much. Is it normal for a droid," he hated using that term, "to remember everything about the woman who created him? And I do mean everything, Aeron. Ask me something about our past. After all, you are the one wanting to stand here and play twenty questions."

She gritted her teeth and grabbed a crystal paperweight off the table nearest her. Aeron pitched it at him with remarkable precision. Extending his arm, he plucked it out of thin air with ease and tipped his head. "You weren't aiming at me, were you?"

She shook her head, pointing at him. "Dead space. You're arrogant to boot."

He'd never seen this side of Aeron and found it difficult to concentrate on much beyond how hard his cock was. She was even more beautiful when worked up. A fire burned in her blue eyes. It was all he could do to remain stationary and not sweep her off her feet. The very thought of burying his cock in her nearly overtook him.

Brad stretched his neck and tried to override his sensory systems to regain control of his lower extremities, particularly the one between his legs. It didn't work.

Wonderful, she gives me the ability to shut off pain but I can't get an erection to go down. Some space age warrior I am. A hot blonde can bring me to my knees. He tapped his foot. *In her defense, she had no clue my reproductive organs are operational. Hell, she wasn't even aware I was operational.*

The corners of his lips twitched at the irony of it all.

Aeron hurled another object at his head. He caught it and tossed it onto the circular sofa.

"You think this is funny?" she asked. "How do you even have a sense of humor?"

"Two chickens walk into a bar…"

She growled and he laughed. "Not funny, Brad!"

"Probably because I didn't get to the punch line yet. There was a wealth of humor files in your databases. As with most of the data, it's from 'Original Earth Files', but amazing nonetheless."

In an instant Aeron was rushing in the opposite direction. Her speed was no match for him and she knew it. She pushed a table over in his path and he leapt, clearing it with ease, catching her around the waist a second before she would have accessed the receiving room doors.

Aeron stiffened in his arms. "Are…you… going to hurt me?"

"No. I've said as much."

"Then let me go," she whispered, the sound of her soft voice nearly breaking his resolve.

He drew in a deep breath, attempting to harden himself to her wiles. "That I can't do."

"Why?"

"Because I want you to understand I would never…"

Something cold and hard pressed against the back of his head. "Let go of her or the Vanos will be picking pieces of your head out of Aeron's upholstery for lunar cycles to come, asshole."

Aeron grabbed hold of Brad's hand as she faced the opposite direction. "Conell?"

"Aeron, you okay?" Conell asked, his eyes holding the anger she remembered seeing flashes of back in school.

Brad let out a low growl. "She's fine. I would never harm my wife. Ever."

"There's the thing, *Brad*, I'm not buying she even is your wife. I'm not even buying you are Fairbanks. Something is off. I don't know what, but I do know Aeron isn't acting like herself."

"You don't even know her anymore, Ballou," Brad said, his teeth clenched.

"Conell, please…go. I'm fine." Aeron's attempt at getting Conell to leave was admirable, but Brad knew it'd be ineffective.

He pressed his lips to Aeron's ear. "Honey, he won't go because he senses the Vanos blood in me. I'm positive, because I sense it in him as well. It's something adult male Vanos can do. It's also why he doesn't believe I'm the Brad he once knew. What he doesn't understand is that he only grew into his Vanos abilities since we last met, so he wouldn't have smelled it in me back then."

Aeron's tiny gasp did the trick. Conell pulled the weapon away from Brad's head for a fraction of a second. It was all the time Brad needed. He thrust Aeron out of the line of fire and spun quickly, sweeping Conell's legs out from under him and securing the P893-G pulse gun. It was Star Union issue and Brad had little doubt Conell's brother had armed him. He admired the scientist for having something to protect himself with and for risking his life for Aeron's, even though hers was not in jeopardy. There was a time in his life that Brad never dreamed Conell would step up to the plate. Seeing him now proved how wrong he'd been about the man. That being said, he wasn't going to let him back into Aeron's life as anything more than a friend. He'd meant what he'd said— in his eyes, Aeron was his wife. He leveled the weapon on Conell and smiled. "It was unwise to hold a gun to my head, Doctor."

Conell narrowed his gaze on him. "Whatever they're paying you to kill her, I'll triple it if you just leave."

What the hell?

Brad's brow furrowed. "No one is paying me to do a thing. I'm here because my wife is here and no one will harm so much as a hair on her head. You had her once, Ballou, and you lost her. I love her and I'm not going anywhere."

A tiny choked noise came from Aeron and he knew her well enough to know his proclamation of love startled her.

"Brad, please don't hurt him," Aeron said, pushing her tiny frame against his body. "Conell meant well."

"Is this guy for real, Aeron? Is he really your husband? Is he Fairbanks?"

Aeron slid her hands over his neck and placed a chaste kiss on Brad's cheek. He was just about to let his guard down and kiss her the way he'd longed to when he felt her going for his cranium chassis. No part of him wanted to believe Aeron would try to shut him down—not that she even could.

Locking gazes with her, he remained still, waiting to see if she would try. Her bottom lip quivered as her eyes glistened. The pain on

Aeron's face was too much for him to bear. He closed his eyes, awaiting her attempt at shutting him down. When it didn't come, he peeked out at her. A lone tear ran down her cheek.

"Brad wasn't hurting me, Conell. We had a minor disagreement and I overreacted. He didn't want me to hurt myself. He knows how nasty my temper is and how I tend to be irrational. That's all. I'm sorry you had to witness this." She drew in a ragged breath. "And yes, he's part Vanos. I know. He's never hidden it from me."

Conell rose to his feet slowly. "You know he's got Vanos blood in him and you still…"

Brad put his finger on the trigger and waited for Conell to comment further. When he didn't, Brad nodded. "The two of you share a rather intimate history, and Vanos blood courses through your veins. How am I any different?"

Aeron coughed and shook her head. It was clear she had an ample list of differences, but didn't share them. "Can we stop this? Please? I don't care about your lineage. I care about protecting the weak. You two aren't the ones killing humans. You're protecting them."

"Aeron?" Conell asked. "You knew the truth?"

She offered a soft smile as she put her hand on Conell's. "It's okay, Conell. I've suspected as much about you from the moment we met. I don't hate the Vanos. They aren't all to blame. I hate what their military is doing to humans. Now, if we could put the weapons away and get along, I'd be a happy girl."

Brad eyed Conell cautiously, wondering what the man would do. Killing him would hurt Aeron, but he refused to lose her to him. "Doctor?"

"My apologies. It was a misunderstanding." Conell extended his hand. "Truce?"

Brad was well versed in the art of etiquette, though he saw little reason for it. Still, he shook Conell's hand all the same. "Truce."

"Oh, Fairbanks?"

"Yes."

"I'm still pissed that you used to steal my lunch chip," Conell said, laughing softly.

"Not half as pissed as I am that you made it to Aeron's heart first, but I'm willing to let bygones be bygones, if you are."

Conell arched a brow. "Do you really love her?"

"The fact you're still alive because she cares for you should be answer enough," Brad said, pulling Aeron into his embrace.

FIVE

Once Brad was positive Conell had not only left the vessel, but had departed from their area of space, he focused his attentions back on Aeron. He'd expected her fear of him to return once Conell was gone. It didn't. Much to his surprise, Aeron hadn't stopped following him around the ship. Granted, she kept a safe distance from him, but still, she trailed behind, observing his every move.

Stopping, he glanced over his shoulder and fought the urge to smile when Aeron pretended to be interested in the latest *Interstellar Update* instead of him. She bit at her lower lip and it was all he could do to remain in place. Tossing her to the floor and having his way with her, while appealing, was unwise at the moment.

"Aeron?"

She jumped slightly and stared at him from wide eyes. "Yes?"

"You can relax, get cleaned up, do whatever. I'd like to head planet-side and check out Perseus first hand. I'll be gone the majority of the day, so it's up to you whether or not you abandon me or wait here until I get back."

"You want to what?" she asked, not bothering to hide the shock in her voice.

Brad couldn't help but smile. "You want me to help in the fight against the Vanos. I need to do a threat assessment."

"But you could be caught, hurt, killed!" The shock on her face warmed him.

"I'll be fine. You saw to it that I have more than I need in training. Though I had a great deal to start with." He headed towards one of the many transport shuttles the vessel had and paused when he sensed Aeron following him. "Aeron, honey, I swore to you that I'd never harm you. You don't have to worry about me sabotaging anything."

"Sabotage?" She gasped. "Brad, I never thought that! I just don't want you to go alone."

Confused, he glanced over his shoulder to find her eyes glistening. "Aeron?"

"What if you don't come back? What if the Vanos discover you? What if…?"

"Then you won't have to fear me anymore and you can build a new droid, assuring the next one can't turn himself on and off." It was a cold statement and he wasn't sure what prompted him to even say it.

Aeron took a tiny step back as her brow furrowed. The pain on her face sliced through Brad, but he didn't apologize. Instead, he continued on his way to a shuttle, being guided by something he couldn't explain. Every ounce of him wanted to hold Aeron in his arms and sample her sweet lips, yet he put one foot in front of the other, leaving her behind. Each step he took, he thought of the visions he'd had of Aeron welcoming him with open arms. The harsh reality was she'd feared him and stumbled through lies to no doubt protect her precious Conell.

I'm jealous.

The realization hit him just as he entered one of the shuttles. Brad knew he should go back, smooth things over with Aeron, but he didn't. He'd been aware of her from day one. She'd only just learned he was more than a mere machine—one of her creations. Time apart would do them good. If she was gone when he returned, then he'd track Conell down and find her. Cutting himself from her wouldn't happen. That much Brad was sure of.

AERON RUBBED HER ARMS, unsure why she'd donned an outfit similar to Brad's before departing for Perseus in another shuttle. She wasn't a solider. Roaming about Perseus without a paid escort or guide was foolish. Chasing the perfect assassin was ludicrous. She didn't care. The need to find Brad and know he was safe was too strong for her to give up and turn back.

The chill of Perseus' pre-dusk air left Aeron shivering as she visually searched the docking station for signs of Brad. She found none. She did, however, find signs of every other kind of life form she could imagine. Some her wildest dreams would have had problems inventing.

She shuddered as she walked past a large blue alien with two heads and six arms. The second she spotted a freakishly long tongue darting out of one of the mouths, she yelped and rushed through the crowd. Fear took hold of her gut, screaming from within at her stupidity for following Brad.

"Dr. Braxton?" a deep voice asked.

She stopped and turned to find an extremely tall male with long, auburn hair. His amber gaze was off-putting at first, but when he smiled, she let her fears lessen. "I'm Dr. Braxton."

"Since I didn't see any other stunning blondes in the area, I assumed so."

She blushed.

He took a step towards her. "Dr. Ballou sent me. He needs to speak with you. It's urgent."

Aeron's heart raced. "Conell? Is he hurt? Did the Vanos…" She eyed the man carefully. She knew Conell had been concerned about the Vanos coming for them both. Her chest tightened. No part of Aeron wanted to believe they truly had come back for them so soon. In her gut she knew better. "Did the enemy find him?"

The man inclined his head. "Yes."

"Is he hurt?"

"Yes and he needs your help."

Instantly, Aeron broke down in tears, the stress of her day catching up with her before she could prepare or address the nagging feelings in the back of her mind.

Something was off.

She pulled herself together, the tears stopping though her cheeks wore their marks. She eyed the stranger. "What happened? Exactly."

The man's gaze narrowed and the edges of his lips twitched with something akin to anger.

He's a threat.

Aeron took a small step back, wanting distance between herself and this man who was up to no good. He reached out quickly, yanking her to him, his grip strong and tight.

Pain shot up her arms.

"Let go of me," she bit out. "I'll scream."

His look was almost daring. "Do it."

She opened her mouth as if to screen.

"Behave, Doctor." He rubbed her back but there was no mistaking the tension in his body. "I'll take you to Ballou. If you're a good girl."

Aeron thought of the ways she could try to

break free. None of them were very brilliant, nor would they work. But she had to at least try. She was about to stomp on the man's foot when something pulled on her.

She was suddenly ripped free from the stranger's grasp. She found herself standing behind a mass of black and watching in horror as Brad picked the auburn-haired man up by his throat. The sheer power Brad exhibited was enough to shock anyone. He made the act appear effortless. Sure, she knew his strength was enhanced, but it was entirely different being witness to the events unfolding.

"You dare to touch her? To think you can lure her away with your lie?" he asked, spit flying as he did. The muscles in his arm flexed and the man he was holding gasped for air, clinging to Brad's wrist but making no progress at gaining his freedom.

Lure me away? "What? Brad, no!"

Brad glanced at her and it cost him greatly. The man pulled a weapon from behind him and pressed it to Brad's chest. Brad loosened his hold on the man.

The man drew in a deep breath as his gaze hardened. "Very good. Now you will die along with her. It matters not to me. The contract allows for additional kills."

Time seemed to slow as Aeron watched history repeat itself. Visions of cradling Brad's head to her long ago as she tried to put pressure on his wound, flooded her. She couldn't do it again. She couldn't watch the man she loved die for her. Once was too much. A second time would do her in. Vaguely she heard someone screaming, only to realize it was her. She snapped back to reality, rooted in place by fear.

Brad's reaction to the weapon pointed at his chest was so fast Aeron almost missed it. He had the man disarmed and lying dead at his feet in a nanosecond. He spun the weapon around his finger before putting it in the back of his pants. A crowd had gathered, no one seeming surprised by the sight of a dead Vanos. Two men stepped forth, patted Brad on the back and went about removing the dead body.

Brad leveled his chocolate gaze on her. He didn't look pleased. In fact, he looked deadly. She squeaked as he came at her, sweeping her off her feet and tossing her over his steely shoulder.

"It is time you learn a few things, wife."

"B-Brad?" she asked, bouncing against his unforgiving shoulder.

He slapped her backside and growled. "I'm in charge here, Aeron. Not you. And it's high time you understood all of what and who I am."

SIX

Brad deposited Aeron on the circular white sofa in the receiving room and kept his tone even when he spoke. "Undress."

Aeron's brows drew together. "What?"

"You heard me," he said, puffing his chest out a bit for effect. "Take your clothes off, now."

"Why?"

"Because I have waited fourteen years to feel you and I refuse to wait another second."

"Fourteen years…but I only began building you… Ohmygod, you've been aware from the get-go."

He didn't respond. He didn't need to. Aeron's facial expression said that she understood she hadn't been alone like she'd assumed. The second tears formed in the corners of her eyes, Brad knew she'd also put together the fact he was her Brad—the Brad she'd assumed was lost.

He wanted to give in and hold her, but needed to know she'd never put herself in harm's way again. He kept the façade of an iron will in place. "Take your clothes off or I will show you how well-trained I truly am, Dr. Aeron Braxton-Fairbanks."

Brad watched her fingers shake as she pulled her shirt up and over her head, freeing her breasts and making his cock rock hard. When she undid her pants and slid them down her slender legs, he thought he would ejaculate right where he stood. He'd watched her get naked every night for years and had even watched her masturbate, but never before had she undressed knowing he was watching her. It turned him on to the point of pain. If he didn't ram his dick into her soon, he'd blow a fuse or go find something to shoot. Neither was a good option.

When she was completely naked, she met his gaze. "Are you planning on hurting me?"

"No," he said, horrified she'd think he could

cause her harm. "I plan on using your body until you can no longer resist your feelings for me."

"Use me for what? You have all my knowledge already."

"I want to fuck you, Aeron. I have wanted to fuck you from the moment I met you in the atrium all those years ago."

She gulped. "But you can't...I mean, your body can't work like that anymore."

"There is much you do not know about me. Now, touch me." He put his hand out to her and watched as she lifted her hand tentatively. When her hand was directly before him, he grabbed her wrist gently, and put her hand over his heart.

"It beats for you, Aeron. It always has."

His sensors read her vitals and determined she was moving from fear to excitement. That was a very good thing.

Brad pulled Aeron to him, and bent his head down. He'd wanted to give her a real kiss for fourteen long years—one that would curl her toes—and now he finally had his chance. She hesitated, before parting her lips enough for his tongue to slip in. His cock ached to be in her and he could deny it no longer. Reluctantly, he drew away from their kiss and unfastened his pants. He pushed them down until they fell the rest of the way off. He kicked them away and ripped his T-shirt off. Pulling her closer to him, he licked his lips before pressing his turgid flesh against her stomach. "I love you, Aeron."

She tensed up. "But you can't…you don't…droids don't love. You didn't love me before, Brad. You don't now."

Feeling no need to argue the point with her, he dropped his hands down to her butt and picked her up. He'd show her how very wrong she was. Careful not to use too much strength, he eased her legs around his waist. Her wet sex pressed against his abdomen and he could think of nothing beyond entering her. "I'm going to fuck you now and you will enjoy it. I promise."

Aeron moaned and dropped her head back as he lifted her slightly and settled her on the tip of his dick. She squirmed in his arms a bit before leaning forward and kissing his jawline. He froze.

"If this is a dream, don't wake me," she whispered. "I missed you so much. So very much."

She wants me too.

Blinded by need, he pulled on her hips, impaling her quickly onto his hard cock. She cried out in his arms and clutched his back. "Too big…ahh…Brad, you're too big."

Afraid of hurting her, he ran a diagnostic scan of her body. His cock's girth spread the walls of her pussy taut, but he could sense no damage being done, so he didn't stop. Besides, from what he could tell, he also stroked her Gräfenberg spot with each thrust, thus causing her as much pleasure as it caused him. After a few more slow strokes, Aeron's pussy began to cream and he slid in and out of her with ease.

"Does it still hurt?" he asked softly.

"No." She kissed his lips and slid one hand into the back of his hair. For a split second he wondered if she'd try to shut him off. When she fisted his hair and bit at his lower lip, he lost control, pumping into her body like a possessed man.

Aeron continued to claw at his back as she moaned. Thrusting his hips upwards, he drilled into her with short strokes as he laid down with her, never allowing himself to leave her body.

He barrel-rolled their bodies, leaving Aeron on top.

She gasped, her eyes wide. "Oh, Brad…ohh, this makes you go even deeper. You feel even bigger."

"Do you wish me to terminate this encounter?" he asked, waggling his brows as he spoke in his best impersonation of a droid. "Do you want it to end, Aeron?"

"Terminate?" Her eyes widened. "No, I want you to fuck me until you can't fuck me anymore."

Her response made him chuckle. Brad pushed so hard that Aeron's tiny body lifted almost clean off him. Not wanting to harm her, he eased up a bit on his thrusts, still enjoying the feel of her hot cunt.

When he felt her pussy clenching down around his shaft, he knew she was coming. The first time of many, he hoped.

The feel of her pussy milking him was too much, his cock twitched once within her as his balls drew up. His orgasm hit him before he could even compute it. Semen shot into her silken depths. Wave after wave of it followed. When he'd modified his semen in the lab, he'd made his body come harder than that of a normal humanoid male. The need to assure he would be able to reproduce with Aeron was great.

Aeron pushed on his chest as he continued to fill her with his seed. "What's going on? Brad, what the hell is that? How are you coming?"

He responded by pulling her down towards him and pressing his mouth to hers as his body continued to empty its seed into her receptive womb. Minutes passed and he thrust his hips once more, still coming, and felt another orgasm tear through her body. The added sensation only helped to prolong his marathon-long ejaculation.

For months he'd tweaked his reproductive system to allow him to control the duration in which he released semen, and how many sperm, if any, were in it. Wanting a family with Aeron for so long had made him decide to lift his sperm levels off the chart for this session. Running his diagnostic scan, he knew she was ovulating, knew she was ripe for him. He let the remainder of his semen leak into her before he stopped thrusting.

It would take sixty seconds for his body to

replenish the amount of semen he'd used, and he wanted to be sure to restock. Now that his first mission was complete, he intended to pleasure himself every way possible with her and make her love him as much as he loved her.

SEVEN

Aeron wiggled on Brad, still unsure if she was awake or dreaming and no longer caring. He felt so good in her, almost like he'd been made just for her. In a way, he had been.

The fact that he could not only ejaculate, but ejaculate longer than a human male was an amazing development. It was also a tad unnerving. She kissed at his lower lip as he began to move beneath her again. "How are you still hard?"

He smiled up at her and melted her heart. "I can control how long I'm erect now...most of the time."

"Most of the time?"

For a second, he looked embarrassed. "I

have found there are certain times when I can't get my erection to dissipate, especially after watching you masturbate. At times, I've had to pleasure myself to alleviate the pressure. Trust me, baby, jacking off to your image is the only thing that kept me from ravishing you all these years."

Her blue eyes widened. "You watched me…?" She couldn't have been more mortified if she tried. How many nights had she lain there, stroking her own clit and fingerfucking herself? Too many to remember.

"Aeron," he whispered, pulling her down to hug her. "I want to watch you do it again and again. Just as I want to take you in every way I've dreamed of."

"Every way?" she asked, still unsure where he'd learned the ones he knew already.

"Yes. I plan on fucking that sweet mouth of yours, tasting your pussy and fucking your tight little ass."

Panic welled up in her. "My ass? No, I've never."

"I will take you in whatever ways I wish and you will accommodate. Am I clear?" His voice was powerful and she knew better than to cross him, not that she even wanted to.

"Brad?"

His expression softened a bit. "Yes?"

"Would you really hurt me?"

He pressed his mouth to hers and slid his tongue in. He traced tiny circles around her own, making her already wet pussy cream more. He ran his hands through her hair and gave it two quick tugs. She jerked back and shook her head, the reality of it all setting in.

"It's you, isn't it?" she asked, already knowing the truth.

He nodded.

Guilt tore through her as she slid off him quickly. "I'm sorry, Brad. You were hurt because of me."

He reached for her but Aeron batted his hand away. "No. I can't apologize enough. You suffered because of me. Now you feel like you owe me. Like you have to give me this because I'm..."

"What?" he asked, shooting up and snaking his arm around her waist. He had her flipped onto her back before she could blink and was staring down at her with a heated gaze. "You think I'm with you right now because I feel like I owe you? Honey, you've got no idea how many years I dreamed of this…of holding you, being in you, telling you how I really feel. You will not take this from me, Aeron. I won't let you trivialize and compartmentalize this like you do everything else."

"But—"

He cut her protest off by capturing her lips with his own. Running her hands up and over his broad shoulders, Aeron found the back of his thick neck and held tight to it as he continued to kiss her. The second he broke the kiss, Aeron moaned, wanting him back. Brad had other ideas. He began to plant tiny kisses on her collarbone as he worked his way lower. As his tongue ran over the swell of her breast, her nipples hardened in anticipation. He drew one into his warm mouth and began to roll it with his tongue to the point her stomach tingled and her back arched.

"Brad."

"You taste even better than I thought you would, Aeron." He focused on her other nipple, giving it equal attention.

On the verge of coming by simply having

her nipples sucked on, Aeron reached out and clawed at the sofa. "Stellar stars, please fuck me."

Brad chuckled and that caught her attention. He really was her Brad. The man she'd fallen for without ever having a real kiss from him. Everything about him continued to surprise her. Moving down more, he began to kiss her lower abdomen. He stroked it gently and looked up at her with loving eyes. "I will fill you with my child—our child."

Instantly, Aeron's chest tightened. She couldn't tell him it would never happen, that he'd never be able to reproduce. The sheer determination in his eyes told her he seriously wanted to create life with her but it wasn't an option. Droids did not reproduce—not even droids who retained their humanity.

"Brad, we can't…"

He parted her slit, cutting her protest off as he slid his tongue over her clit. Aeron held tight to his shoulders as he licked her swollen nub, eliciting tiny bursts of pleasure. The second he added his fingers, pushing two into her cunt and fucking her with them, Aeron abandoned thoughts of explaining they could never reproduce and gave in to the thrill of having Brad back with her.

"Mmm," he murmured against her pussy, alternating licks and sucks.

Her inner thighs tightened and an involuntary spasm left her clamping them against the sides of Brad's head. A manly chuckle followed as her orgasm struck. Brad stayed there a moment, lapping up her cream before rising over her, his mouth glistening.

He lined up with her and drove in to the hilt. Aeron arched, countering his thrusts. She wrapped her legs around his waist, allowing him to go deeper.

"Uh." He pumped harder. "Aeron, you feel so good."

Brad kissed her and she tasted herself on his lips. It spurred her on, bucking against him, loving the feel of him. Loving him.

Another orgasm struck, causing her pussy to contract around his shaft. Brad tossed his head back, growling as he rooted deep in her, filling her completely with his come.

EIGHT

Brad stared down at Aeron's sleeping form. He'd literally worn her out to the point she'd fallen asleep before he even withdrew completely on their sixth joining. He'd carried her to bed and wiped away traces of their combined juices so she could rest in comfort. Prior to the accident, he'd never thought of himself as a man who would enjoy cuddling any female, but that's what he'd done for the last several hours. He'd held her close to him, listening to her soft, rhythmic breathing and steady heartbeat.

"I love you," he whispered, bending to kiss her forehead.

She turned in her sleep towards him. "Mmm, I love you too, Brad."

Closing his eyes, he fought the urge to wake her and smother her in kisses. It was hard. Hearing her reaffirm what she'd confessed so many years prior was a dream come true.

He sighed. The dream would shatter soon enough if what he suspected was true. The man in the marketplace claimed Conell sent him. There was no way in hell Conell would ever harm Aeron. The man adored her. Always had and most likely always would. He'd grown from an awkward, skinny geek to a man with the ability to survive when need be. The universe had hardened him, but one thing Brad knew for sure, it hadn't hardened him to the point he'd ever willingly hurt Aeron. The Vanos were notorious for their torture techniques and could extract information from almost anyone. The very fact the Vanos knew of Aeron meant the information came from Conell. Brad's refusal to believe the man could turn on Aeron left only one thing—Conell had been captured.

He shuddered at the thought of Conell being tortured. He might always have a jealousy issue in regards to the man, but in the end Conell was someone he'd once called a friend and he couldn't allow him to be held by the Vanos.

Aeron would follow if she knew he was going planet-side again and he couldn't risk her being harmed. Especially not now.

He raked his gaze over her glorious form, letting it rest on her lower abdomen. If what he suspected was true, she was with child or would be very soon, depending upon when conception actually took place.

"I'll be back, honey. I promise."

With that, he did the hardest thing he'd ever done in his life—he walked away from her.

NINE

Orbiting Planet Perseus in the Prometheus Quadrant of the A-QPT45 System
Five months later…

AERON MOVED SLOWLY between the rows of hydroponic plants she'd been tending to in order to maintain some sense of sanity. It wasn't as easy as it used to be. No. She now had to contend with a swollen stomach and persistent, low-back pain. The baby growing within her was a miracle. The fact that his father had walked out on her five month ago, after one night of passion, was bittersweet. Brad had left her with a broken heart and his child. Regret wasn't an option.

She glanced out the viewing port at the planet below and bit back emotions that wanted to run free. She'd sworn she'd never return to this quadrant again, but found herself plotting a course for it all the same. Normally, she'd change in mid-route, but this time was different. This time, she kept going.

Already, she'd been in orbit above the planet for close to two weeks, awaiting news on a guide to take her around. Her central notification computer beeped, indicating an incoming call.

"Yes?"

"Aeron?" Kiwi, a young female she'd befriended two months prior, asked. She'd been docked near Aeron's ship in another quadrant, injured from a Vanos attack. Aeron aided her, rebuilding the damage the Vanos had done. "I have news."

"Did you find me a guide?" she asked, hopeful.

"Umm, not exactly. Can I dock?"

Aeron snorted. "Of course you can, Kiwi. You're always welcome here. You know that."

"I'll, umm, meet you in the receiving room in five," Kiwi said, shutting communications down.

Odd.

Aeron set her potting shovel down and made her way toward the bay doors. It would take her at least five minutes to make it to the other side of the ship. She went as quickly as possible, wondering what in the universe made Kiwi act so strange.

"Give her a bit, boy."

The sound of Kiwi's voice carried down the corridor. "You are an impatient one, aren't you?"

Wondering who Kiwi was talking to, Aeron rounded the corner and came to a dead stop. There before her was Brad. He was being blocked by the petite brunette with a temper to rival his own.

Kiwi had her hands on her hips and was facing the other direction. "I know you're claiming to be her husband, but like I already told you, if you hurt her in any way, I'll tear your dick off and cram it up your ass."

Aeron couldn't say she was shocked to hear something like that fall from Kiwi's lips. The girl had a tendency to spit out whatever was on her mind. She *was* shocked to see Brad. He hadn't changed a bit in five months.

He looked past Kiwi and spotted her. His dark gaze went to her swollen stomach. "Aeron? Honey?"

Instantly, every emotion she'd felt for the past five months surfaced. Tears fell freely as she clenched her fists. "How dare you *honey* me? You vanish," she tossed her arms in the air, "with no warning, no goodbye, nothing, and you think you can show up here and *honey* me?"

Kiwi punched Brad in the gut. Since Kiwi used the arm Aeron had rebuilt, giving it droid qualities, Brad actually doubled over. Seeing him in pain silenced her anger, making way for worry.

She rushed to his side and touched his arm gently. "Brad, you're hurt."

"Only…my…pride," he bit out, his gaze going to Kiwi. The minute he looked at Aeron, it softened. He drew her into his arms and held her close.

"You left me," she whispered, still in tears, but holding tight to him.

"*Shhh*, honey." He kissed the top of her head and gave the braid she wore two quick tugs. "I never meant to be gone so long."

"Why?" Aeron asked, unable to get out all

of what she wanted to know. Why had he left her at all? Why had he been gone so long? Where had he been? Hadn't he loved her enough to stay with her?

"Can we come in now, or are you still going to tear vital pieces of us off too?" a deep, familiar voice asked.

Kiwi grunted. "Maybe. It depends on what Aeron wants. I've been itching to hit you since we were planet side. Give me an excuse, big guy."

"Big guy?" the voice echoed, a hint of suggestion in its tone.

"Conell?" Aeron drew back slightly, still holding Brad but looking around him now. When she spotted the tall blond wearing fatigues, she gasped. "Conell? What the hell happened to you? You look like a…a soldier."

Brad chuckled. "Told you she'd be more surprised to see you donning military gear than to see you."

"You're laughing?" Aeron stared up at the man who had broken her heart. "Are you telling me that you've been with Conell this entire time?"

"He saved my life, Aeron," Conell said,

moving to stand near Kiwi. "He knew the Vanos had captured me. He even went and got himself captured to gain access to the prisoner camp."

Aeron drew in a sharp breath before smacking Brad in the arm. "You did what? You've had training in every possible scenario and you get caught that quickly?"

A sheepish smile spread over his face. "I got caught. On purpose."

"Bradshaw Fairbanks, I cannot believe you'd run off and—"

He swept her off her feet and pressed his mouth to hers, silencing her protest. The feel of his tongue dancing around hers was too much. Aeron gave in and kissed him back, savoring his sweet taste. Tiny moans escaped them and she heard Kiwi making slight gagging noises.

Conell's laugh had her and Brad pulling back slightly. Brad didn't put her down though, keeping her close to him. The baby picked then to kick, nailing his father in the process. Brad's gaze snapped to hers. His eyes widened. "I never meant to be gone so long, Aeron. I love you and our child. Never did I think when I went to find Conell that I'd be gone from you for months."

It was on the tip of her tongue to ask why it had taken so long to get back to her.

"He saved my life too," a new voice said.

"And mine."

"Mine too," another called out.

"Same here."

Kiwi sighed and looked as if she was trying not to laugh. "See a pattern here? I know I did when they told me the story."

It continued, and Aeron patted Brad's shoulders for him to put her down. He refused, but was kind enough to turn so she could see who was talking. When she spotted a group of men and women filing in from Kiwi's cargo ship, she shook her head, the reality of it all sinking in. "They were *all* prisoners?"

"Most," Brad said. "Some are Vanos defectors—men who don't believe in what their government is trying to force them to do. I told them they'd be welcome here with us, Aeron."

She nodded, stroking his cheek while she stared at everyone. "Of course."

Conell winked. "Hey, Fairbanks, have your wife check you over. I think your wiring must be damaged. You don't have her in your bedroom, making love to her like you swore you'd do the minute you got home to her."

"Pig." Kiwi snorted. She didn't sound nearly as disgusted as Aeron guessed she wanted to.

Conell grinned from ear to ear. "Why, thank you, little lady."

For a moment Aeron was sure Kiwi would lay into Conell as well. She didn't.

"You were all Brad went on about for months," another man said, laughing. "Ma'am, that man loves you more than life itself. Hell, if I could have figured out a way to shut him down, I would have, just long enough to get a day without him talking about how much he missed you and how much he wanted to get home to you and his baby."

Aeron froze. They knew Brad was part droid?

Brad chuckled. "Calm down, honey. Most of them are too. They were in bad shape. It's why it took me so long to make it back to you. I had to rebuild them, grow organs and care for them just as I watched you do for me all those years. We were locked up and couldn't make our escape until everyone was well enough to travel." He motioned towards the Vanos men in the group. "They were kind enough to smuggle supplies in for us and to help us hide what we were doing from the other guards. They hated seeing us used as slave labor almost as much as we hated being used."

Conell turned in a slow circle, with his arms out. He appeared to be in the best physical shape of his life. "Half is me, half isn't. Your *husband*," he put emphasis on the word, "refused to leave my side until I was healed. He then told me everything, Aeron. We worked to heal the others and then overthrew the guards and left. The last month has been spent trying to locate you. When Kiwi showed up looking for a guide for a feisty, determined blonde doctor with a 'bun in the oven' we knew she meant you."

"Yeah, you're a regular Einstein," Kiwi bit out. "People will flock from quadrants far, far away to catch a glimpse of your brilliance."

"Yes." Conell stepped closer to Kiwi. "But the question is, what would you like to catch a glimpse of?" It was certainly a loaded statement.

Aeron didn't miss the way Conell's gaze seemed to linger over Kiwi or the heat that flared on her friend's face. Kiwi looked away and took an unnatural interest in her shoes. Conell boldly stared at her, not seeming to care who saw him. A little piece of Aeron hoped Conell would find happiness someday soon. He deserved it.

She tossed her arms around Brad's neck, hugging him tight. "You have five seconds to get me to our room before I unleash Kiwi on you."

Kiwi flexed her rebuilt arm and winked. "Say the word."

Brad grinned and kissed the tip of her nose. "I only need two." With that, he rushed with inhuman speed towards their quarters. Laughter echoed in the halls behind them. As the bay door slid shut, Brad captured her mouth with his once more, kissing her with a passion that left her breathless.

"Brad," she whispered, kissing the edges of his mouth.

He wiped her cheek and came away with a tear. "I'm here now, honey, and I'm not leaving you again." Sliding his hand down, his gaze locked with hers as he palmed her swollen stomach. "Either of you, Aeron."

She knew better than that. "Brad, we both know you'll fight for the cause."

He nodded. "I will, but I won't be gone for months again." A waggle of his brows and a sly grin told her Brad was feeling cocky. "Thanks to you, I'm incredibly efficient in everything I do. I'll kill them quicker so I can get home and love you."

"Promise?" she asked, knowing he spoke the truth, but needing to hear him agree.

"I promise, honey." He walked her towards their bed and kissed her forehead gently. "Now, what do you say we make up for lost time?"

Aeron giggled, relishing the feel of being held by him. "Mmm, ready to prove how efficient you truly are?"

"Always, Doctor. Always." He smiled. "I love you, Mrs. Fairbanks."

"I love you too, Bradshaw."

THE END

Dear Reader

Did you enjoy this title and want to know more about Mandy M. Roth, her pen names and all the titles she has available for purchase (over 100)?

About Mandy:

New York Times & *USA TODAY* Bestselling Author Mandy M. Roth is a self-proclaimed Goonie, loves 80s music and movies and wishes leg warmers would come back into fashion. She also thinks the movie The Breakfast Club should be mandatory viewing for...okay, everyone. When she's not dancing around her office to the sounds of the 80s or writing books, she can be found designing book covers for New York publishers, small presses, and indie authors. She also writes as Reagan Hawk, Kennedy Kovit and Rory Michaels.

Learn More:

To learn more about Mandy and her pen names, please visit http://www.mandyroth.com

For latest news about Mandy's newest releases and sales subscribe to her newsletter

To join Mandy's Facebook Reader Group: The Roth Heads, please visit

https://www.facebook.com/groups/Mandy-RothReaders/

Review this title:

Please let others know if you enjoyed this title. Consider leaving an honest review on the vendor site in which you purchased this title. Reviews help to spread the word and boost overall sales. This means more books in the series you love.

Thank you!

Lightning Source UK Ltd.
Milton Keynes UK
UKHW01f1818250718
326289UK00001B/149/P